THE PUPPY PLACE

HONEY

ELLEN MILES

LITTLE APPLE

SCHOLASTIC INC.
New York   Toronto   London   Auckland   Sydney
Mexico City   New Delhi   Hong Kong   Buenos Aires

For Dog, who has always loved a good dog joke

ISBN-13: 978-0-545-08349-2
ISBN-10: 0-545-08349-4

Cover art by Tim O'Brien
Original cover design by Steve Scott

12 11 10 9 8 7 6 5 4 3 2 1   9 10 11 12 13 14/0

Printed in the U.S.A.

First printing, January 2009

CHAPTER ONE

"Whoa, Buddy!" Charles tightened his grip on the leash. Buddy might only be a puppy, but he sure was strong! He was barreling down the sidewalk, towing Charles along behind him.

"He can't wait to see his sisters," said Sammy.

"Maybe," Charles said doubtfully. "But I think it's just that Buddy's always in a hurry. It's like my dad's favorite joke: This dog is wolfing down his food, eating as fast as he can, and his owner says, 'What's your hurry? Late for your nap?'"

Sammy cracked up. That was the nice thing about having Sammy for a best friend, thought Charles. He always laughed at Charles's jokes. Charles laughed at Sammy's jokes, too. In fact, the two boys were writing a joke book together!

First it was going to be called *101 Funniest Dog Jokes*, but then they found out that there already was a book with that name. So now it was *102 Funniest Dog Jokes*.

"That could be joke number ninety-eight!" Sammy said. "We're almost done!"

"Except for the pictures," Charles said.

Both boys groaned. Neither of them was that great at drawing dogs. Sammy could draw dinosaurs and airplanes, and Charles could draw school buses and dump trucks. But dogs were hard. And the joke book would be *so* much better with pictures.

Sammy said the book would be a bestseller and that they'd be rich. Charles wasn't so sure. But honestly, he didn't really care. He just liked to think up jokes and write them down.

Just then, Buddy pulled at the leash again. This time, he wanted to sniff a tree. Buddy sniffed and sniffed. And sniffed. And then he sniffed some more. Charles stood there, trying to be patient.

Finally, Buddy lifted his leg and peed. Then he looked up at Charles.

What're we waiting for? Come on! Let's go!

And Buddy forged on ahead, pulling Charles behind him. Charles shook his head and smiled. Buddy sure was silly sometimes. But Charles loved his little puppy more than anything in the world. Buddy had soft brown fur and big brown eyes and a heart-shaped white patch on his chest. Buddy had come to stay with Charles and his family as a foster puppy, but he had ended up becoming a permanent part of the Peterson family. All the Petersons loved Buddy: Lizzie, Charles's older sister; the Bean, his little brother (whose real name was Adam); and Dad. Even Mom, who was usually more of a cat person, had fallen in love with Buddy.

The Petersons had fostered lots of puppies who needed homes. That meant that they had given each puppy a safe, happy place to live until they could find it the perfect forever family. The very first puppy the Petersons had fostered had been adopted by Sammy and his parents, next door. That was Goldie, a golden retriever. She and Buddy were best friends, just like Charles and Sammy.

"Maybe Buddy *is* excited about seeing his sisters," Charles said to Sammy now as Buddy towed him along. It was true that Charles had told Buddy that they were going downtown for a special reason on that bright, sunny Saturday morning in February. Charles had explained to Buddy that they were going to have a family reunion at the Lucky Dog bookstore. Not a Peterson family reunion. No, this was Buddy's *dog* family.

When Buddy had first come to the Petersons', he had arrived along with his doggy mother and two sister puppies. That was the first time the

Petersons had fostered a whole dog family. It was a challenge to find homes for them all, but everything worked out in the end.

Jerry Small, who owned the bookstore, had adopted Skipper, the mother dog. She had a great life, since she got to hang around the store every day. All the bookstore customers loved Skipper. She was a star! Cocoa and Cinnamon, Buddy's sisters, had been adopted by Mary Thompson. Mary was a real, live author. In fact, she was famous for a book called *So Many Puppies*. The amazing thing was, Cinnamon and Cocoa looked just like the puppies in that book. So it was perfect that Mary had decided to give them a home.

Once in a while, Mary called the Petersons to suggest a get-together. It was always fun to see the three puppies playing together, while Skipper stood nearby looking proud of her growing babies. Mary had called that morning, and everybody had agreed right away that it was time for a visit. Since Lizzie was busy volunteering at the animal shelter, Charles got to take Buddy downtown.

Was it possible that Buddy really *did* understand about seeing his family? Sometimes, when Charles or Lizzie asked, "Do you want to see Cinnamon and Cocoa?" Buddy's ears would perk up and he would tilt his head from side to side as if he were considering the question. But of course Buddy also did that when you asked, "Do you want a treat?" or "Are you a good boy?" or even, "Who's a big silly-head?"

The truth was, Buddy was a happy pup who was always eager to go wherever anybody wanted to take him. Sometimes he went down to the firehouse with Charles's dad, who was a firefighter. Sometimes he went to the newspaper office with Charles's mom, who was a reporter. Once Buddy had even come to school, so Lizzie could demonstrate while she gave an oral report on dog training. Mom had brought him, and she said

Buddy walked right up the front steps as if he'd gone to school every day of his life! He had even poked his nose into room 2B, Charles's classroom.

"Well, here we are!" said Charles as the boys arrived at the bookstore. "Your favorite store, Buddy!" All dogs were welcome at Lucky Dog Books. In fact, Jerry Small even had a bulletin board full of pictures of his "regulars," dogs who visited frequently. And he always kept a jar of especially good dog biscuits behind the counter. Like all the other dogs, Buddy knew just where those treats were. He pulled hard on his leash, dragging Charles right through the door and over to the counter.

"Hello there, Buddy!" said Jerry, who was standing behind the cash register. He dipped his hand into a big glass jar and pulled out a few biscuits. Skipper must have heard the jar opening, because she came trotting right over from her spot near the store's coffee bar.

Buddy and Skipper crunched their biscuits, then started to sniff each other, tails wagging. Buddy put his paws up on Skipper's shoulders and started to nibble on her chin.

"Where are Cinnamon and Cocoa?" Charles asked Jerry.

"I bet that's them right now," the store owner answered as the bell over the front door jingled.

Sure enough, in walked Mary Thompson. She held two green leashes in her right hand. Cinnamon was at the end of one, and Cocoa was on the other. And in her left hand, Mary held a red leash. A tall, lanky puppy with shiny golden-yellow fur dashed around her feet, tangling the red leash with the green ones and nearly tripping Mary.

"Who is *this*?" Charles asked, kneeling down to gather all the puppies into a big hug. The yellow puppy climbed right up into Charles's lap — even

though she was way too big to be a lapdog! —
and began to lick his face all over with her rough,
pink tongue.

"This is Honey," said Mary Thompson. "She's
almost a year old. She's smart and sweet and
wonderful — and she needs a home!"

CHAPTER TWO

"You're kidding!" Charles looked up at Mary. "This puppy needs a home? But she's so cute! Who would ever give her up?"

Now the puppy was chewing on Charles's earlobe. It tickled so much that Charles laughed out loud.

Mmmm, delicious! I like the way this person tastes! And he's laughing, so that means it makes him happy when I do this. I guess I'll do it some more!

Buddy, who was probably a little jealous of all the other puppies, tried to climb over Honey so he could chew on Charles's other earlobe. Mary

10

let Cinnamon and Cocoa off their leashes so they could join in. Charles fell over onto the store's carpeted floor. Giggling, he opened his arms and the puppies climbed all over him, chewing and licking and snuffling and wagging their puppy tails. Skipper came over and joined in, pawing at Charles's arm for attention and touching noses with each of her puppies in turn.

"Puppy pile!" yelled Sammy, throwing himself down next to Charles. Soon he was covered in puppies, too.

Mary and Jerry laughed. "I think they're all happy to be together," said Jerry.

"Nothing like a puppy reunion," said Mary.

Finally, Charles sat up and caught his breath. He threw his arms around Honey and kissed the top of her soft, golden head. "Does this puppy really need a home?" he asked.

Mary nodded. "Honey belonged to a friend of mine. The whole family loved her, but now they have the chance of a lifetime — to move to London,

England! If they wanted to bring Honey, she would have to be in quarantine for six months."

"Quar-what?" asked Sammy.

"Quarantine. That means she would have to be kept away from any other dogs, in case she had some sort of illness. She would have to live in a kennel, away from her family."

"But she looks like such a healthy dog!" said Charles.

"She is, but that doesn't matter," Mary told him. "It's just the rule. And my friend couldn't stand the idea of putting Honey in a kennel for that long. She thought *I* should adopt Honey. She said Honey belonged with my puppies, because they all have 'food' names."

Mary shook her head. "I tried it for three days. Honey is a good girl. She's been to puppy kindergarten and obedience classes. Her family taught her excellent manners and socialized her well with other dogs and people. She's nearly full-grown. But she is still definitely a puppy. And there is absolutely no way I can handle three rambunctious puppies. Cinnamon and Cocoa keep me busy enough."

Charles could understand that. As his mom said, even one puppy was a real handful sometimes. "Well," he said, "maybe we could foster her. I mean, my family." He gave Honey a squeeze. It would be so much fun to have her come to stay at his house.

Mary lit up. "That was just what I was hoping you would say!" Then she smiled nervously. "Um, in fact, do you think you could possibly take her today? I have company coming over for dinner and I just can't imagine how I'll get everything done with three puppies underfoot."

Charles bit his lip. "I don't know . . . I'd have to call my mom."

But Sammy was shaking his head. "Forget about calling!" he said. "Take her! You know your mom won't be able to say no once she sees this puppy."

13

Charles rolled his eyes. Sammy was always full of wild ideas. Like when he thought they should hypnotize Charles's mom into agreeing to keep Goldie, when she first arrived. Or when he wanted to go ghost hunting at an old abandoned house.

But the truth was that some of Sammy's ideas were good, too. And Charles had a feeling his friend was right this time. After all, who in the world could look at a puppy as cute as Honey and not want to keep her around, at least for a little while? At least until they found her the perfect home.

He nodded. "Okay," he told Mary. "We'll take her."

Mary looked relieved. "Really? That's wonderful!"

Jerry Small seemed concerned. "Are you sure, Charles?" he asked. "I'd be happy to let you use the phone if you want to call home."

But Charles wasn't even listening anymore. He had his nose buried in Honey's soft, sweet-smelling fur and he was hugging her close. There was no way he would let Mom say no to this puppy. They just *had* to foster her. In fact, maybe they could even keep Honey forever! She would be the perfect pal for Buddy.

"Right, Buddy?" Charles asked, reaching out to pull his own puppy into his lap. The two puppies touched noses and snuffled at each other happily. Charles could tell they would get along beautifully.

Cocoa and Cinnamon wanted to be part of the fun. They climbed into Charles's lap, too. Then all four puppies clambered down and jumped onto Sammy. Then they chased one another all around the bookstore, with Skipper trotting after them. Finally, the galloping pups knocked over a display, sending dozens of books tumbling to the floor.

Jerry let out a loud whistle. "Maybe that's enough puppy playtime for today," he said.

"Yes, I need to get home and get dinner started."

Mary scooped up Cinnamon and Cocoa and clipped on their leashes. Then she bent down and gave Honey a big hug and kiss. "I'll miss you, cutie-pie," she said. "But I just know you're going to love the Petersons." Honey squirmed happily and wagged her tail.

I love everybody who's nice to me!

Charles found Honey's leash and snapped it on. "Can you take Buddy?" he asked Sammy.

As the boys left the store, dragged by two eager puppies, Charles heard someone call his name. "Hey, Charles!"

Who was calling him? Charles turned around and saw a tall, skinny boy walking toward him. It was Harry! Harry was one of the coolest guys around, a high-school baseball star who drove an old red convertible. Also, he was really nice. Charles had gotten to be friends with Harry when Harry's aunt and cousin had adopted Princess, a

16

spoiled little Yorkshire terrier that the Petersons had fostered.

"Hi, Harry!" Charles loved having a chance to show off his cool older friend to Sammy.

Then he saw who Harry was with.

CHAPTER THREE

"Quick, pick Buddy up," Charles told Sammy. At the same time, he shortened Honey's leash so that she was standing right next to him. He put his hand on her collar. "We don't want to distract that working dog." Charles had spotted a big brown dog — he had a feeling Lizzie would say it was a chocolate Lab — wearing an orange vest that said SERVICE DOG. The dog was walking between Harry and a pretty girl who was gliding along in a wheelchair.

"Charles, my man!" Harry held out his hand for a high five as soon as he was close enough. "How's it going?"

"Great!" said Charles. Honey was struggling to pull away and say hello, but once he'd smacked hands with Harry, Charles got a good grip on the puppy and held her close. She wriggled all over and wagged her tail and gave Harry a big puppy grin. "This is our new foster puppy, Honey," Charles said. "And that's my friend Sammy, with Buddy."

"And this is my girlfriend, Dee, and her pal Murphy." Harry patted the big brown dog's head as he spoke. "What are you guys up to?"

"We were just having a puppy reunion at the bookstore," said Charles. "Buddy got together with his sisters and his mom."

"Cool." Harry reached out to scratch Honey's ears. "This girl is adorable."

Charles knew Harry was a dog lover. In fact, he had a wonderful chocolate Lab of his own, a big, goofy guy named Zeke. "Where's Zeke?" Charles asked.

"He's just chilling at home today. Sometimes he's kind of a bad influence on Murphy when they're together." Harry smiled down at Dee.

Dee smiled, too. "Murphy knows he's not supposed to play when he's on duty, but who can resist Zeke?" Her hand was resting on Murphy's back. Murphy sat calmly and gazed up at her with his big golden-brown eyes. When Dee said his name, his tail wagged gently. Murphy was watching every move Dee made. Charles could tell that this girl and her dog were very, very close.

"What kind of service dog is Murphy?" Charles asked. "I mean, what does he do?"

"Want a demonstration?" Dee's eyes were twinkling. "Murphy loves to show off."

"Definitely!" Sammy spoke up before Charles could even answer.

"Yeah!" Charles agreed.

Dee winked at them. Then she reached down and gently shoved her pocketbook off her lap. "Oops!" she said as it plopped onto the sidewalk.

Instantly, Murphy jumped to his feet, grabbed the pocketbook very gently with his teeth, and laid it carefully on Dee's lap. Then he sat down again and gazed up at her face.

"Good boy," said Dee. Murphy's tail gave that little wag again.

"Wow!" said Charles. "That was awesome!"

"Really cool!" agreed Sammy. "What else can he do?"

"All kinds of things," said Dee. "Since I can't walk, it's great to have Murphy's help with things like carrying packages or getting something off a counter for me. He can help me balance as I'm getting in and out of my wheelchair, and if I fall he can help me get up. He knows how to turn on lights and open doors and how to help me dress and undress. One of his favorite jobs is helping me pull off my socks! He even helps me make my bed every morning." She turned to look at her dog. "Don't you, Murph?"

Now the big dog's tail was wagging harder. Charles was sure that he knew Dee was talking about him. Murphy even let out one big woof, as if to say, *That's right! I sure do!*

"My mom would love that!" said Sammy. "I never remember to make my bed. How do you teach a dog to do that?" Charles could tell Sammy was thinking about teaching Goldie to make his bed, too.

"To tell you the truth, I don't know!" said Dee. "I wasn't the one who trained him. I got him through a group called Best Friends Service Dogs. Murphy went to school for a long time to learn how to do all those things. But you know what? The most important thing about Murphy isn't all the special jobs he can do. The most important thing is that he *is* my best friend, and he's always there when I need him. Right, Murph? You're my best pal, aren't you?"

Murphy stood up and gave another big woof. Now his tail was wagging like crazy.

Honey woofed back.

Hi! You look like you'd be a good friend to have. I sure would like to sniff you!

Honey's bark was like a smaller version of Murphy's. She squirmed and pulled at the leash, straining to get closer to the big dog.

"It's okay," said Dee. "Go ahead and let her say hello."

"Buddy, too?" asked Sammy, who was having trouble hanging on to the pup in his arms.

"Buddy, too," said Dee. "Murphy will let them know if they're bugging him too much. He's not shy."

Charles and Sammy let the puppies go over to Murphy, carefully holding on to their leashes. Honey was bigger than Buddy, but both puppies were quite a bit smaller than big, strong Murphy. The two smaller pups practically tumbled over themselves, rolling on the sidewalk so their pink bellies showed. They wriggled happily as Murphy sniffed each one in turn. Then they both jumped on him at once, attacking him playfully. Buddy nipped at Murphy's front legs while Honey chewed on his ear, his neck, his nose — whatever she could grab.

Murphy put up with it all for a few minutes. Then Charles saw him put one big paw on top of Buddy's back. Murphy also opened his big jaws wide and gave Honey a soft, warning play-bite. Both pups backed off quickly.

"See? Murphy knows how to handle puppies." Dee was laughing as she watched her dog take control. "He knows how to say, 'Enough is enough.'"

"That Honey is really something," said Harry. "How long have you had her?"

Charles gulped. "About half an hour," he admitted, suddenly realizing that his mom and dad did not even know yet that there was a new foster dog in the Peterson family. "We better go!" he said to Sammy. "Nice to meet you," he told Dee.

Charles gave Murphy a pat on the head. "And your cool dog."

"See you!" Harry said, giving Charles another high five.

"Hey, we should invite these two to our party," Dee said to Harry. She turned to Charles and Sammy. "Want to come?" she asked. "We're having a Valentine's Day party at the Fairview community center on Wednesday afternoon. Nothing mushy-gushy, just cupcakes and games and things. You'll meet a few other people who have service dogs, too."

Charles thought it sounded like fun. "Sure," he and Sammy both said.

"Great! See you then. And good luck with finding a home for that sweet Honey!" she added as the boys walked away.

CHAPTER FOUR

"Forget about good luck finding Honey a home," Charles said to Sammy as they walked back to his house. "First of all, I need good luck finding out if this puppy even has a *temporary* home with my family."

"Don't worry." Sammy waved a hand. "Trust me, it'll all work out."

That did not really make Charles feel any better. The truth was, you could not always trust Sammy to use what Charles's mom called "good judgment." But it was a little late for Charles to remember that now. The boys were headed home, with Honey and Buddy trotting ahead of them down the sidewalk. Honey's ears were perked up on alert, her tail was high, and she looked happily from side to side, checking out everything and everybody she passed. She sure was cute. Charles could hardly imagine his mother making him bring Honey back to Mary Thompson.

When they got home, Mom's van was not in the driveway. But Lizzie was back from working at the animal shelter. "Hey!" she called. "In here!" Lizzie was curled up on the couch in the living room, reading a book. If Charles had to guess, the book was probably about dogs.

Lizzie sat straight up and let the book drop to the floor when she saw Honey. "Oh, she's adorable!" she cried, reaching a hand out for Honey to sniff. "Are you shy, little yellow Lab girl?"

Lizzie always knew what breed a puppy was. She'd learned a lot from that "Dog Breeds of the World" poster in her bedroom. She also usually guessed right about whether a puppy was a boy or a girl.

"Her name's Honey. Think Mom and Dad will let us foster her?" Charles asked.

Now Lizzie was patting her lap, inviting Honey up. Honey scrambled onto the couch and tried to fit herself onto Lizzie's lap. "Of course they will!" Lizzie said. "How could they resist?"

"Where *is* Mom, anyway?" asked Charles.

"She went to Mrs. Pritchard's to pick up the Bean," Lizzie said. Mrs. P. was the Bean's new babysitter. Lizzie held Honey's head in her hands. "Oh, look at that face! I'm going to go get the camera!" Gently, she helped Honey back onto the floor. Then she reached down to pick up Buddy. "Love you, too, little guy." She kissed his nose, put him down next to Honey, and ran out of the room.

Mom came home about one second later. She had the Bean in her arms. His head was resting on her shoulder and his eyelids were almost shut.

"Mom —" Charles began.

But Mom put her finger over her lips. "*Shhh!* I'm going to let him sleep a little more so I can finish an article I'm working on." Then she spotted Honey. "Oh, my!" she whispered. "That's a big puppy! Did Lizzie bring it home for us to foster?"

Charles shook his head. He was just about to admit that *he* had brought Honey home, when Mom said, staring at Sammy, "Yours, then? I can't believe your parents agreed to another dog!"

Then, before either boy could say a word, she was off up the stairs with the Bean.

Charles and Sammy looked at each other.

They shrugged.

"Oh, well," said Sammy. "It's not as if you told her a lie!"

"No," said Charles glumly. "But I'll have to tell her the total truth really soon. And then it'll look like I *did* lie, even though it wasn't my fault."

Just then, Lizzie came down with the camera. She started shooting pictures while the boys helped pose the dogs. First they tried to make

Buddy and Honey sit next to each other nicely, but of course that didn't work since both puppies just charged over and tried to lick Lizzie and the camera. Then Charles gave Buddy a knotted rope tug toy, and soon Honey had grabbed the other end. The pups pulled and tugged, trying to get the toy away from each other. Then they ran around the room, each holding one end of the toy, wrestling and tumbling and growling little puppy growls.

Lizzie, Charles, and Sammy were laughing so hard they could hardly breathe, when Charles heard Mom calling from upstairs. "Lizzie! Can you go check on the Bean? I hear him calling for me but I'm just trying to finish this paragraph."

Lizzie groaned. "I guess I'll read his Froggy book to him for the billionth time," she said. "That usually keeps him quiet for a little while." She handed the camera to Charles and headed upstairs.

Charles and Sammy kept playing with the

pups. Now Buddy was teasing Honey by showing off his plush yellow duck toy. He tossed Mr. Duck in the air and ran after it, batting at it with his paws so it almost seemed alive. Honey dashed after Buddy, trying to grab the toy. She chomped on to the end of one wing and tugged so hard that Charles heard something rip. "Whoa there!" he said.

Oops! I didn't mean to break it!

Honey let go of Mr. Duck and looked up at Charles. She lay down and rolled over so her tummy showed, just like she had when she met Murphy.

Forgive me?

"That's okay," Charles said. "You didn't mean to. You're just a big, strong puppy, that's all."

Instantly, Honey rolled back over, jumped to

her feet, and grabbed Mr. Duck before Buddy could get him.

Charles heard the Bean yelling. He heard his little footsteps pounding down the upstairs hall, toward Mom's office. But the puppies were so much fun that he pretended not to hear. Finally, Mom called, "Charles! Can you come help Lizzie? Maybe if you can get him to play monkey-face, the Bean will quiet down. All I need is five more minutes."

So Charles left Sammy in charge of the puppies and went upstairs. He found Lizzie and the Bean in Mom's study. The Bean was trying to climb into Mom's lap. Mom was still trying to type on her computer.

"Hey, look at me!" Charles said from behind Mom's chair. He squooshed up his face like a monkey's. Then he made some hooting noises and pretended to scratch under his arms. The Bean usually loved that and stopped whatever he was doing to watch and laugh and imitate Charles.

But this time the Bean wasn't quitting. "Mama! Come *on*, Mama!" he yelled, pulling on Mom's arm. He wailed and wailed. Then he made a "poor little puppy" face, with big sad eyes. He held his hands up under his chin, pretending they were paws, and began to whimper the way Buddy did when he wanted a treat. (Sometimes the Bean liked to pretend he was a dog.)

Finally, Mom gave up. "Okay, sweet pea." She lifted the Bean onto her lap. Instantly, he stopped yelling. "Let's go downstairs and see Sammy's new puppy, shall we?" She turned back to Charles. "That sure is a cute puppy! I almost wish we were fostering it ourselves!"

"Well," Charles began, "in that case, I guess I have some good news for you."

CHAPTER FIVE

Charles had to admit that his mother was a really good sport about the whole thing. When he had explained the misunderstanding about where Honey had come from, Mom had laughed. "Well, it's partly my fault," she'd admitted. "I was just in such a hurry to get back to work on my article." Then she had bent down to give Honey a big smooch on the nose. "And she *is* just about the cutest puppy ever," she said, quickly adding, "except for Buddy, of course!"

She and Dad had agreed that very night that the family could foster Honey. Mom had also agreed to drive Charles and Sammy to Fairview for the Valentine's Day party — "as long as I get to babysit Honey while you're there!"

Charles was telling all of this to Harry and Dee that Wednesday. He and Sammy had gotten to the community center early, and they were helping Dee blow up pink and red balloons — the finishing touch on the decorations. "Mom really loves that puppy," Charles said, shaking his head.

"Well, who wouldn't?" asked Dee.

"You don't understand," Charles said. "My mom has always been more of a cat person. She doesn't usually go bonkers over our foster puppies. Except for Buddy, of course." He tried to tie off the end of his pink balloon, but it was blown up too big. He let out a little air.

"So, maybe you'll get to keep Honey forever!" Harry said. He took the balloon from Charles and managed to tie a knot. "That would be cool."

"That would be awesome," said Charles. "Honey is the sweetest puppy! She's so mellow and mature. Not like some of the nutty puppies we've fostered." As they blew up more balloons, Charles told Dee and Harry a little bit about Rascal, the jumpy Jack Russell terrier, and Pugsley, the mischievous pug, two of the wildest puppies the Petersons had cared for. "Honey's not like them," he explained. "She doesn't bark, or jump on people, or lick the insides of their nostrils." Sure, she liked to play with Buddy, galloping at full speed around the house, but that was just normal puppy behavior. "And she's not spoiled at all, like Princess was." Charles and Harry grinned at each other.

"I didn't have Murphy as a puppy," said Dee, "but my friend Mimi who works for Best Friends told me he was like that, too. Very mellow, very easy to take care of." She smiled down at her big brown dog and bopped a balloon toward him. Murphy bumped it gently with his nose and it flew back toward Dee.

"He even knows how to play catch!" Sammy exclaimed. "Murphy, you're the best!"

Murphy's tail thumped on the floor.

"Okay," said Dee. "I think we have enough balloons. Anyway, it looks like some of our guests have arrived!"

Sure enough, the community center was filling up. Charles saw three or four kids riding around in wheelchairs. One girl had a very cool red scooter that Charles wanted to get a closer look at. He also saw two service dogs in orange vests, a black Lab with the girl in the scooter and a beautiful, big golden retriever with a boy in a wheelchair. Lots of other kids were running around, tossing balloons at one another, and checking out the tables full of cupcakes, cookies, and punch.

"We get a good crowd for our parties here," said Dee. "They're sponsored by our town's Center for Independent Living, where disabled people help one another. But all kinds of people come to our parties, because they know we always have a good time. Come on, I'll introduce you to some of my friends while Harry hangs up those balloons."

First Dee introduced Sammy and Charles to

Dakota, the girl with the scooter. Her black Lab was named Boomer. She had gotten him from Best Friends, too. He was really friendly. Dakota explained all about how her scooter worked. Then the boys met Steven and his golden retriever, Kramer, who was also from Best Friends. Kramer was amazing! He could pick up anything, including a set of keys or a dollar bill, and give it back to Steven.

"And you probably know Noah," Dee said as she and the boys approached the food tables. "He goes to your school, doesn't he?"

Charles did recognize the boy in the wheelchair who was helping himself to a pink cupcake. He'd seen him rolling down the halls plenty of times, and out on the playground. "Hi," he said. "I'm Charles."

"You're Lizzie Peterson's brother, aren't you?" the boy asked. "She's in my class."

"You're *that* Noah!" Charles realized he'd heard all about this boy. "The artist, right?"

"Well, I don't know about that," said Noah modestly.

"Definitely, he's an artist," said Dee. "Noah can draw anything!"

"Yeah, didn't you win the Fire Prevention Week poster contest?" Sammy asked.

"He's won it every year since he was in kindergarten," Charles said, before Noah could answer. "Lizzie talks about you all the time. I just didn't know —" Charles stopped, embarrassed.

"You didn't know I was in a wheelchair?" asked Noah. "Great! I'd much rather be known for being good at art or for a wacky haircut or something. Who wants to be 'that kid in the wheelchair'?"

"Noah, why don't you show them some of your pictures?" Dee asked. "I have to go refill the punch bowl." She winked at Charles and Sammy, told them not to eat too many cupcakes, and rolled off with Murphy trotting behind her.

Noah pulled a notebook out of a pocket on the side of his wheelchair and flipped through it, showing Sammy and Charles dozens of beautifully detailed drawings made with colored pencils.

"They're all of dogs!" Charles said. Sure enough, there were great pictures of Murphy and Boomer and Kramer, plus lots of other dog drawings.

"I love dogs," Noah told him. "They're definitely the funnest thing to draw."

Sammy leaned in to take a closer look at the pictures. "Wow. Look at that Great Dane! You are really, really good."

"It's no big deal," said Noah. "It's simple. I could probably teach you guys how to draw dogs, if you want. I'm here after school almost every day. Come hang out, and I'll give you a lesson!"

Sammy and Charles looked at each other and grinned. Charles knew they were thinking the same thing. Maybe, with Noah's help, they'd be able to finish their joke book after all!

CHAPTER SIX

Drawing lessons started the very next day. Charles and Sammy arrived at the community center with paper, pencils, and erasers. They had also brought along pages and pages of dog jokes, all the ones they had collected so far.

The place was a lot quieter than it had been the night before. Dee and Murphy weren't there, and neither were any of the other kids who had service dogs. A few middle schoolers were doing homework together at one long table, and two girls giggled together in a corner where a bunch of pink balloons still bobbled.

The boys each grabbed a heart-shaped cookie — party leftovers that had been put out on a plate — and took over one of the other tables.

41

It turned out that Noah loved jokes as much as they did! He laughed as he read the first few jokes they showed him. Then he told one of his own. "What do you get if you cross a sheepdog with a rose?" he asked.

Charles and Sammy shook their heads.

"A collie-flower!"

All three boys cracked up. "Good one," said Charles.

"Joke number ninety-nine!" said Sammy.

"Here's how you could illustrate that joke," said Noah. He bent over his lap desk and drew a few quick strokes on a piece of paper. Suddenly, the picture came to life and Charles saw a collie's head coming out of a rosebush!

"How do you *do* that?" Sammy's eyes were huge.

Noah shrugged. "Try it," he said. "It's not so hard. See, first you make a triangle, then put a circle here, then add this oval part and the two triangles that will be his ears. . . ." He drew as he talked, and another dog began to come to life on the page.

"Slow down!" said Charles, who was scribbling madly on his own paper. "Wait!"

Noah went over it again. "First a triangle, then a circle..." He drew more slowly, and Sammy and Charles tried to copy every stroke. But when they'd finished, only one of their drawings actually looked anything like a dog. Noah's.

Sammy groaned. "I'll never get it!" he said.

"It just takes practice," Noah said. "Keep trying. If you do different shapes, you get different dogs. Like, a long oval makes a wiener dog." Quickly, as if it were nothing, he sketched a dachshund wearing roller skates.

Charles frowned down at his own paper. His circles and triangles and ovals just looked like a mishmash of scribbles, like something the Bean would draw. He sighed and turned the paper over. Then he started again.

"Tell me more about Honey," Noah said while they drew. He had been really interested the night before when Charles and Sammy had told him about the Petersons' new foster puppy. "Is her nose black or brown?"

"Black," said Charles. "And her eyes are really dark brown, so dark they almost look black. And she has these long, dark eyelashes."

"She sounds pretty." Noah bent over his drawing.

"She has this big, goofy smile," added Sammy. "She always looks happy, just like my puppy, Goldie."

"Honey is smart like Goldie, too," Charles said. "She's already learned to pick up after the Bean!" He laughed. "Every time he leaves a sock or a toy somewhere, Honey picks it up and brings it to him. And you should see the size of her paws. They're huge! Lizzie says that means Honey is going to be even bigger than she already is, when she's full-grown."

Charles looked down at his drawing. Another mess. He crumpled up the paper before Noah could even see it, and started over.

Sammy crumpled up his paper, too. "Argh!" He sounded frustrated.

"Relax," Noah said. "You have to just let it flow naturally."

"Easy for you to say," grumbled Sammy. But he took another piece of paper and tried again.

"What else about Honey?" Noah asked.

"When she's hungry, she goes over and bangs on her food dish," Charles reported. "It's hilarious. She bops it with her paw in this certain way so it turns up on its edge, then she pushes it around the kitchen with her nose until somebody feeds her."

Noah laughed. "Dee tells me stories like that about Murphy, too. He's such a smartie."

"Isn't Murphy the best?" Charles asked.

"He is." Noah nodded. "Maybe someday I'll have a service dog like him."

Suddenly, Sammy put down his pencil. "Hey!" he said. "What if Honey could be your service dog?"

Noah's mouth fell open. "Wow!" he said. "That would be — just so totally amazing. But — I don't think I'm old enough."

"Old enough?" Sammy looked confused. "You're older than me and Charles, and *we* both have dogs."

"But, Sammy —" Charles put down his pencil. "Wouldn't Honey have to get trained and stuff?"

"Sure, but Lizzie could probably do that." Sammy waved a hand casually. "She knows everything about training dogs."

Charles remembered when his family had fostered Shadow, a black Lab who was now in training to be a guide dog for a blind person. He knew it was a little more complicated than Sammy was making it sound.

"Plus, didn't Dee say that the most important part about Murphy was that he was her best friend? Honey could be Noah's best friend starting today, without any training at all!" Sammy was really excited now.

Then Noah moved his arm, and Charles's eye fell on the drawing he'd just finished. "Oh, wow!" He could hardly believe his eyes. Noah had drawn a boy in a wheelchair — a boy who looked just like Noah — with a dog wearing a SERVICE DOG vest standing next to him. "How did you do *that*?" Charles asked. "You never even saw Honey, and that dog looks exactly like her!" It did, too. Down to the big paws and the dark eyes and the goofy smile.

Noah shrugged. "You described her, didn't you? I feel like I already know her." He tore the picture off his pad and handed it to Charles. "You can have it, if you want."

That did it. All of Charles's doubts about Sammy's idea flew out the window. "You know what?" he asked Noah. "Sammy's right. You and Honey belong together. We'll figure out a way to make it happen. I promise!"

CHAPTER SEVEN

"You *what*?" Lizzie glared at Charles. Her arms were crossed and her mouth was a straight line.

Charles looked away, then down at the floor. "I — I promised," he mumbled. "I promised Noah that Honey could be his service dog." He had thought Lizzie would be happy. She loved it when they found perfect homes for the puppies they fostered.

Charles had just told Lizzie all about Noah's drawing, and about how much Noah wanted a service dog of his own. And about how he, Charles, had made a promise he might not be able to keep. Charles didn't know why, but Noah had seemed to take the promise seriously, even though Charles was only a kid.

Lizzie shook her head in disgust. "What were you thinking? Do you really think it's that easy? Don't you remember what we went through with Shadow? Have you gone out of your mind? How disappointed do you think Noah will be if this doesn't work out?"

Did Lizzie really want him to answer all those questions? Charles didn't know where to start. By now, he realized that he had probably made a big mistake. But he hadn't *meant* to. Now he was going to have to tell Noah that it might not work out after all. And there was no way he could avoid Noah. The boys had made plans to go together to a big wheelchair basketball tournament, and it was only two days away.

"I didn't —" Charles began. He reached down to pet one of Honey's soft ears. She and Buddy had just been tearing around the living room, and now they were both taking a quick nap between play periods. Honey had laid her head on Charles's lap and fallen asleep instantly. She was so soft and warm! Now she lifted her head. She seemed to understand that Charles was upset, and she licked him gently on the cheek.

It's okay! Don't worry! Everything will be fine.

Lizzie threw up her hands. "You didn't think, that's what." She sighed. "Honey's a wonderful dog. But even though she's almost full-grown, she's just a puppy. She can't be anybody's service dog right now. First she would probably have to spend some time with puppy-raisers — like the Downeys, the family that raised Shadow, remember?"

Charles did remember. The puppy-raisers' job was to help the puppy grow into a happy dog. Puppy-raisers were supposed to teach puppies their manners and make sure they grew up strong and safe. But hadn't Honey already been raised pretty well? She might only need a little more time to grow up with people who cared about her.

Charles kissed the top of Honey's head. "What if *we* could be Honey's puppy-raisers?" Charles could just imagine how much fun it would be to play with Honey and Buddy every single day, and to watch Honey grow up into a beautiful big dog like Murphy.

"I doubt that could happen," Lizzie said, shaking her head. "Anyway, then Honey would have to go to a training center to learn all the things she would have to know in order to be a service dog." Lizzie crossed her arms again as she went on, interrupting Charles's daydream. "If she makes it through training — and not all dogs do! — then she would be assigned to someone who needs her and who is ready to take care of a service dog. Could that be Noah? Maybe. But that's a long, long way off."

All Charles heard was the "maybe" part. So

there was still a chance! He was not ready to give up on the promise he had made to Noah.

Just then, Mom came into the living room. Charles could hear Dad and the Bean upstairs, getting ready for the Bean's bath. They were singing the alphabet song. The Bean usually only sang it the regular way through G, then after that he liked to put in whatever letters popped into his mind. So Charles heard, "A, B, C, D, E, F, G!" Then, to the same tune, "T, L, B, C, L, B, C!" The Bean loved C, L, and B, since those were letters that belonged to people in his family.

"What's going on?" Mom asked. She came right over and sat down on the floor next to Charles, so she could pet Honey. She looked from Lizzie to Charles. "I could hear you guys arguing all the way upstairs."

"Charles thinks he found a home for Honey —" Lizzie began.

Charles thought he saw Mom's face fall. But

then she put on a smile. "Really?" she asked. "That's — that's great!"

"But he hasn't!" Lizzie went on. "Charles thinks we could be Honey's puppy-raisers, then she could go to Noah as a service dog. He just doesn't understand why that won't work!"

"I'm not sure I do, either," said Mom. She leaned over and nuzzled the top of Honey's head. "I know when we wanted to be Shadow's puppy-raisers, they told us that you guys were too young. But we've fostered so many puppies since then! We have a lot of experience. Maybe they *would* let us be Honey's puppy-raisers!"

Charles and Lizzie looked at each other. They had not seen Mom fall this hard for a puppy since Buddy had arrived. Mom really wanted to keep Honey around for as long as she could.

"I was thinking we could ask Dee for advice," said Charles. "You know, Harry's girlfriend? The one who owns Murphy?"

"Great idea!" Mom agreed.

Lizzie threw up her hands. "Whatever."

Dee and Harry came over the very next night. It took a little work to get Dee's wheelchair into the house; the kitchen door was the only one wide enough. Harry and Dad had to lift the wheelchair up the back stairs. Charles had never thought before about how complicated it must be to do everything in a wheelchair.

"I've been dying to see Honey again," Dee said. She patted her lap, and Honey jumped up to put her paws on Dee's knees.

Hello! I remember you!

Honey didn't seem afraid of Dee's wheelchair at all. Dee stroked the puppy's head gently. Murphy sat next to Dee, as close to her as he could get. His eyes never left her face, even when Buddy batted at his ears and chewed on his chin, trying to get the big dog's attention. Meanwhile, the Bean looked at Dee's wheelchair with big eyes.

Dee smiled at him. "I'll give you a ride later, how about that?"

"'Kay!" The Bean stuck his finger in his mouth and smiled up at her, shy and excited at the same time.

Charles and Mom took turns explaining about how they were hoping that Honey could become Noah's service dog, and that they, the Petersons, could be her puppy-raisers.

Dee listened and nodded, her face serious. "It's a great idea," she said when they had finished. "And I agree that Honey has a lot of potential. She seems so smart and calm!"

Charles and Mom grinned at each other. But Dee had more to say.

"But there's one big problem, right from the start. Best Friends requires their service dog owners to be at least twelve years old — and Noah is only ten!"

CHAPTER EIGHT

The day after Dee and Harry came over, Dad drove Sammy and Charles to meet Noah and his dad at the wheelchair basketball game, which was at a big, fancy college gym in Middle City. The place was packed with fans who yelled and clapped and stomped their feet so hard that the wooden bleachers shook.

"This is so cool!" Sammy said.

"Isn't it?" asked Noah. "I hope I can play like these guys when I'm older."

"They are incredible athletes," Dad said, shaking his head. "It's amazing how they get around. Did you see how that guy managed to pick himself up after his wheelchair went over?"

Charles didn't say anything. He was trying to

pay attention to the game, but he could not stop thinking about what Dee had said. Or about how he was going to break the bad news to Noah.

The action on the court was almost too fast to follow. Charles could not believe how quick the players were. Pushing their wheels with strong arms, they scooted around the court on their wheelchairs faster than Charles could run! Noah had explained the rules. "The main difference between this and regular basketball is that the players can only touch the wheel of their chairs twice between dribbles, otherwise it's like traveling in regular basketball. You know, when somebody takes too many steps without bouncing the ball."

The players had special wheelchairs, very light-weight with special wheels that slanted inward so they could change direction quickly without tipping over. When three guys in wheelchairs surrounded a player with the ball, they could keep him from moving at all! The surrounded player would have to heave a long pass to one of his teammates.

"Which team are we rooting for?" Sammy asked.

"I know a guy on the green team," said Noah. "His name's Justin. He comes over to the community center to coach us sometimes. I have his autograph and everything. That's him right now with the ball! See? Number twenty-five? Let's root for them."

"Go, green!" yelled Sammy, at the very moment that Justin tossed the ball in a high arc toward the basket.

Swish! The ball fell right through the net.

Sammy jumped to his feet. "Yay, Justin!" he shouted.

"Attaway, green!" yelled Dad.

Noah pounded on the armrests of his wheelchair. His dad threw an arm around him and yelled, "Go, Justin!"

Charles wanted to yell and clap and stomp his

feet, but he couldn't. He was still having a hard time concentrating on the game. Why? Because he knew he had to let Noah down. Soon he would have to tell Noah that he, Charles, was not going to be able to keep his promise. Honey was not going to be Noah's service dog after all.

Sure, Dee had said that she would try to think of a solution to the problem. But it was obvious that it was not going to work out. Charles and his family were going to have to find another home for Honey, and Noah was going to have to wait — and wait, and wait! — for a service dog of his own.

Charles felt terrible. And it didn't make him feel any better that Noah had introduced him to his dad as "Charles, the guy who's going to get me my own service dog!"

Noah's dad had grinned and stuck out his hand for a shake. "We've missed having a dog in the family," he said. "I hear this pup you're caring for is a real good one. Can't wait to meet her!" Then he and Noah had told Charles about some of the regular dogs they'd owned in the past. Obviously Noah's family loved dogs and knew how to care for them. What was so different about a *service* dog? Why couldn't Noah's family take care of Honey?

"Yeah!" Noah yelled now. He threw his fist into the air. "Did you see that play? That was an awesome steal!"

Charles had not seen it. He was too busy trying to figure out how he was going to explain things to Noah. Charles was miserable.

At halftime, there was a free-throw contest, open to all kids under the age of fourteen. "Want to try?" Noah asked.

Sammy jumped right up. "I'm in!"

Charles shook his head. "I think I'll just hang out," he said.

Noah's dad and Charles's dad were talking about the game. Charles sat quietly and watched as Noah rolled his wheelchair out onto the court and started tossing a ball around with Sammy and Dakota, the girl Charles had met at the community center. Charles remembered Dakota's service dog, Boomer, a happy black Lab. Noah had drawn some great pictures of Boomer.

Just then, Charles felt a tap on his shoulder.

"Hey, Charles!"

It was Dee, with Harry standing next to her.

"I didn't know you guys were coming!" said Charles.

"Are you kidding?" Harry asked. "We never miss a game. Dee plays in the women's league. She's awesome. You should see her shoot threes."

Dee blushed. "There are lots of good players on my team," she said. "Anyway, listen! I have some news for you. I talked to my friend Mimi, who works for Best Friends, and I told her how much you want Honey to go to Noah."

"You did?" Charles asked. "What did she say?"

"Well, she said I was right about the rules. . . ."

61

Dee paused, smiling. "But she also said that sometimes there are creative ways to work around the rules."

Charles felt himself smiling. "Really?"

"Since you know both of them, she wants you to write her a letter and tell her all about Noah and Honey and why they would be good for each other. Can you do that?" She handed Charles a slip of paper with Mimi's e-mail address on it.

Charles was nodding hard. Maybe things would work out all right after all! "I'll do it as soon as I get home!" he promised.

Dee held up one hand, fingers crossed. "Let's hope for the best!"

CHAPTER NINE

Noah came in third in the free-throw contest, and the green team won the game by just one point — but Charles hardly noticed. Instead of worrying about how he was going to tell Noah that he couldn't keep his promise, Charles had started thinking about the letter he was going to write.

As soon as he got home, Charles went to find Honey. "Come on, sweetie," he said. "I need you for inspiration." Charles grabbed Mr. Duck and showed the raggedy stuffed toy to Honey. She barked happily and wagged her tail as she jumped for it. Holding the toy just out of Honey's reach, Charles carried Mr. Duck upstairs. Honey followed him right into his room. "Good girl!" said Charles, tossing Mr. Duck to the frisky pup. Then Charles lay down on the floor with Honey, and the two of them played tug-of-war for a while. Honey made Charles laugh out loud when she shook Mr. Duck so that his flapping wings smacked her in the nose.

Then it was time to get to work. Charles let Honey have Mr. Duck to chew on. When he sat down at his desk and opened his notebook, a picture fell out. It was the picture Noah had drawn of the boy and his service dog. What a great drawing! "Look, Honey," said Charles, showing it to her. "This is going to be you someday!"

Honey glanced up at him with her mouth full of Mr. Duck. Charles thought she looked like she was smiling.

Whatever you said, it sounds like fun!

"More inspiration!" said Charles, propping up the picture so he could look at it while he wrote.

Then he pulled out a piece of paper and began. Charles liked to write on paper first, then copy what he'd written onto the computer. He made fewer mistakes that way, and never lost what he was writing.

Dear Mimi and all the people at Best Friends Service Dogs, he wrote.

My name is Charles Peterson. My family fosters puppys who need homes. Right now we have one named Honey. She is a yellow Labrador Retreever almost a year old. Honey is very smart and helpful and sweet. She already knows how to pick things up and bring them to you, and she sometimes pulls my brother's socks off so she can do stuff like that, too. She is a good, good girl.

"Aren't you?" Charles turned to look at Honey. "You're a good girl, right?"

Honey chomped on Mr. Duck and made him squeak.

That's me! I'm a good girl. Everybody tells me so.

65

"I thought so," said Charles. He went on with his letter.

I think Honey would be a good service dog. She is mello like Murfy was when he was little. (That's what Dee says.) And I know somebody who needs a service dog. His name is Noah and he can't walk so he has a wheelchiar. He is only ten and I know you have to be twelve. But Noah is very machoor and a good artist too. And his family has had lots of dogs. So they know how to take care of dogs.

Charles shook out his hand. Was the letter getting too long? He had a lot to say.

I know that Honey has to go to puppy raisers and then get trained. But what if we (my family the Petersons) were Honey's puppy raisers and then she could live with Noah while she was getting trained? Then he would have a best friend and he could help train her too.

Squeak, squeak, squeak. Honey was really chomping on Mr. Duck now. "You're silly," said

Charles. He wanted to play with Honey some more, but first he had to finish the letter.

I promised Noah that I would help him get Honey for a service dog. Can you help me keep my promise? Yours sinserely, Charles Peterson.

Phew! Done.

"Charles?" There was a tap at the door and Mom peeked inside. "There you are! And there's my little Honey-pie." Mom swooped into the room and knelt down to hug Honey. She kissed her nose. "Who's my Honey-bunny?" she murmured. Honey squirmed and wriggled and licked Mom's face. Mom laughed as she hugged and kissed the puppy some more. Finally, she looked up at Charles.

He was looking back at her, his eyebrows raised.

"I know, I know," Mom said, blushing. "I just really like this puppy, okay?" She came over to Charles's desk. "What are you working on?"

First Charles thought he would hide the letter. In a way, he had wanted to figure this mess out on his own, without any help. But then he had a better idea. "It's a letter," he said. "Maybe you could help me with the spelling." It was an important letter, and Charles wanted it to be perfect. He explained what the letter was about, and how Dee had asked him to write it.

Mom sat down on the bed with Honey on her lap. She read through the letter. "Good job!" she said. Then she helped Charles find the words that were spelled wrong, and they looked them up in the dictionary. After that, Charles typed it into the computer and e-mailed it to Mimi.

"Let's not tell anybody else until we know more," Charles suggested. This time he knew better than to get anybody's hopes up. Anybody's but his own and Mom's, anyway!

Mom nodded and pretended to zip her lips. "Your secret is safe with me!" she said. "Now all we have to do is wait."

*   *   *

They didn't have to wait long. When Charles got home from school the next day, Mom pulled him into the den. "Guess what?" she whispered. "Mimi came to visit today. She wanted to meet Honey. And she brought Noah's mom and dad with her! She asked a million questions, and they spent a long time with Honey."

"So? Is Noah going to get Honey? Are we going to be her puppy-raisers? What did Mimi *say*?" Charles asked.

"Well," Mom said. "There's good news and bad news."

CHAPTER TEN

"I didn't know you guys were coming today!" Noah looked surprised. "Are you here for another drawing lesson?"

It was the next afternoon, and Sammy and Charles had just arrived at the community center. They had more than one surprise planned for Noah! "Actually, we brought some people we want you to meet," said Charles. He glanced back at the door just in time to see Mom and Mimi walk in. Charles introduced his mom to Noah.

"Hi, Mrs. Peterson," he said.

Mom smiled. "Hi, Noah! I've heard a lot about you."

"And so have I," said Mimi, reaching out

to shake Noah's hand. "I'm Mimi, from Best Friends."

"Oh!" said Noah. "You mean — the service dog people?"

"That's right," said Mimi. "And I have some good news for you, thanks to Charles, who is a very convincing writer."

Noah's eyes lit up when Mimi mentioned good news.

She went on, explaining the plan. "I met Honey yesterday. Just as Charles told us in a letter he wrote, she is an especially mature and well-behaved puppy. In fact, she's almost grown-up enough to start training to be a social dog, without having to go to puppy-raisers first."

Mom and Charles looked at each other with sad smiles. That had been the bad news Mom had told Charles about. They would not get to keep Honey around after all. But the good news that Mimi was about to tell Noah more than made up for it.

"Do you know what a social dog is?" she asked Noah.

"Uh-uh." Noah shook his head.

"Well, sometimes we place a dog with a person who's too young to handle a service dog. That person, his parents, and the dog all train together to become a team. The dog is allowed to go everywhere with the person, except to school, as long as one parent is with them. It's a great program. The person and the dog really have a chance to bond. And all the people they meet get a chance to learn about dogs that help people." Mimi took a deep breath. "Your parents met Honey yesterday, and they have agreed to take on this project with you."

"So, you mean Honey and I will be a team?" Noah was starting to smile. Then he frowned. "But what happens when I get older? Do I have to give her up?"

"Nope." Mimi was smiling, too. "If you guys work well together — and I have a feeling you will — then eventually you will do a whole lot more training together, and Honey will graduate from being your social dog to being your service dog!"

"Because by then I'll be old enough —" Noah began, as if he couldn't quite believe it.

"Old enough to have a service dog of your very own. To have Honey!" Mimi was beaming. "There's just one more thing we have to make sure of. We need to be absolutely sure that you and Honey will get along as well as Charles thinks you will." She turned toward the front door and waved.

Lizzie walked in, with Honey walking proudly next to her on her red leash.

Noah straightened up. "That's Honey, isn't it?"

"That's Honey," said Charles.

Noah's smile was huge. "Honey!" he called. "Here, Honey!"

Hearing her name, the little pup picked up the pace, eagerly pulling Lizzie across the room.

Honey ran right up to Noah and put both front paws up on his knees.

Hello! Hello! I just know we're going to be best friends!

Noah reached out to pat her. "Oh!" he said. "Her fur is so soft! And she's even more beautiful than I imagined." He bent down to kiss the top of her head. "Hello, Honey," he said. "Hello, sweet girl."

Charles felt Mom's hand on his shoulder. He looked up and saw her happy-sad smile. She was going to miss Honey as much as he was — but like everybody else, she could see right away that Honey and Noah belonged together.

Lizzie looked over at Charles and gave him a thumbs-up. "Good job," she mouthed.

"I can't believe I'm finally meeting Honey," said Noah. He kissed her some more. "I can't believe she's going to be my service dog." He looked up at Charles and Sammy. "It's all thanks to you guys," he said. "I owe you big-time. If there's ever anything I can do for you — anything at all —"

"Actually, there *is* one thing you can do for us," said Charles. "We've been meaning to ask."

Sammy nodded. "Since you can draw dogs so well —"

"Would you illustrate our joke book?" Charles finished.

"Full credit!" promised Sammy. "A three-way partnership. You'll be rich, just like us!"

Noah grinned. "I'd be happy to," he said. He stroked his puppy's head. "On one condition: Honey gets to be on the cover!"

PUPPY TIPS

Some people might think it's mean to make a dog work instead of letting it just be a pet. But the truth is, many dogs are happiest when they have a job. Every dog likes to help his or her owner, whether by being a service dog like Murphy, herding sheep like Flash the border collie, or even just showing off a new trick or walking nicely on a leash, as your own dog might do. Give your dog the chance to do something that makes you proud — you'll *both* be happy!

Dear Reader,

Can a dog really be your best friend? Ask anybody who lives with one! Dogs make you laugh every day with their silly ways, and they comfort you when you are sad. They're always up for a game or a walk, or just a quiet cuddle. Dogs are very good at keeping secrets, and they are great at making new friends. They like hugs and kisses and they are happy to share your lunch. Most of all, your dog will always, always love you, no matter what. Now, that's a best friend!

Yours from the Puppy Place,
Ellen Miles